Hugs on the Wind

Marsha Diane Arnold and Vernise Elaine Pelzel

illustrated by Elsa Warnick

HARRY N ABRAMS INC PUBLISHERS

ARTIST'S NOTE

I transfer my pencil drawings to watercolor paper, then lay a watercolor wash. With the shapes established, I erase the pencil, leaving no drawn lines. Layer upon layer of watercolor is painted and blotted, feeling to me like sculpting, as each layer clarifies the forms. I use Fabriano Artistico 140 lb. 100-percent cotton, cold-press watercolor paper. My primary brush is Winsor and Newton Series 7, size 2, and for larger areas, size 4.

Designed by Becky Terhune
Production Manager: Jonathan Lopes

Library of Congress Cataloging-in-Publication Data has beem applied for.
ISBN 0-8109-5968-2

Printed and bound in China
10 9 8 7 6 5 4 3 2 1

Harry N. Abrams, Inc.
115 West 18th Street
New York, NY 10011
www.abramsbooks.com

Abrams is a subsidiary of LA MARTINIÈRE

For family and friends and sweet memories to hold
—M. D. A.

For Onnivin and Brendelyn, to bridge the distance
—V .E. P.

For Greg and Patrick
—E. W.

Little Cottontail looked across the Great Green Meadow, to where the sky touches the grass.

"Mama, I wish Grandfather Cottontail had not gone so far away," he said. "I think he misses me too much."

"I am sure he does," said Mama Cottontail, as she gathered sweet red clover.

"What do you think Grandfather misses most about me?"

"He always loved your snuggly hugs," said Mama Cottontail.

Little Cottontail felt the Wind tickle his ears and ruffle his fur. "I have an idea, Mama! I will wrap my hugs around the Wind. The Wind will blow them to Grandfather, all the way across the Great Green Meadow."

"What a clever Cottontail you are," said Mama.
Little Cottontail made a circle with his arms and
lifted it high in the air as the Wind rushed past.

"What else do you think Grandfather misses?"

"Your smiles always made him happy," said Mama.

Little Cottontail looked up at the bright white Clouds gliding by. "I have an idea, Mama! Cloud smiles can travel miles, all the way to Grandfather. I will send my smiles up to the Clouds."

Little Cottontail looked high into the sky and grinned,
then turned somersaults in the grass.

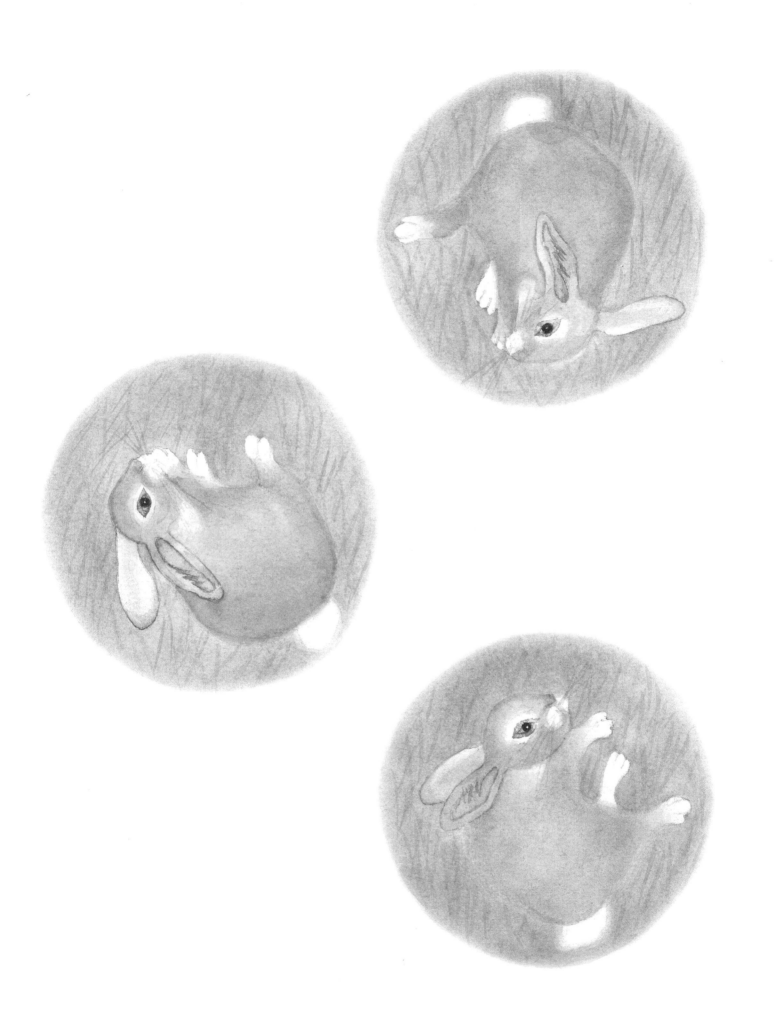

"What else does Grandfather miss?"

Little Cottontail liked this game.

"Remember how he laughed at your jokes?" said Mama, hopping to the River.

Little Cottontail listened to the River as it murmured to the rocks. "I have an idea, Mama! I will tell my funniest joke to the River. The River will carry it to him."

"That is a good idea," said Mama, as she collected wild lettuce.

Little Cottontail leaned over the River's bank and whispered his funniest joke into the water. The River babbled merrily on its way.

"Now the River and Grandfather and I have a joke together."

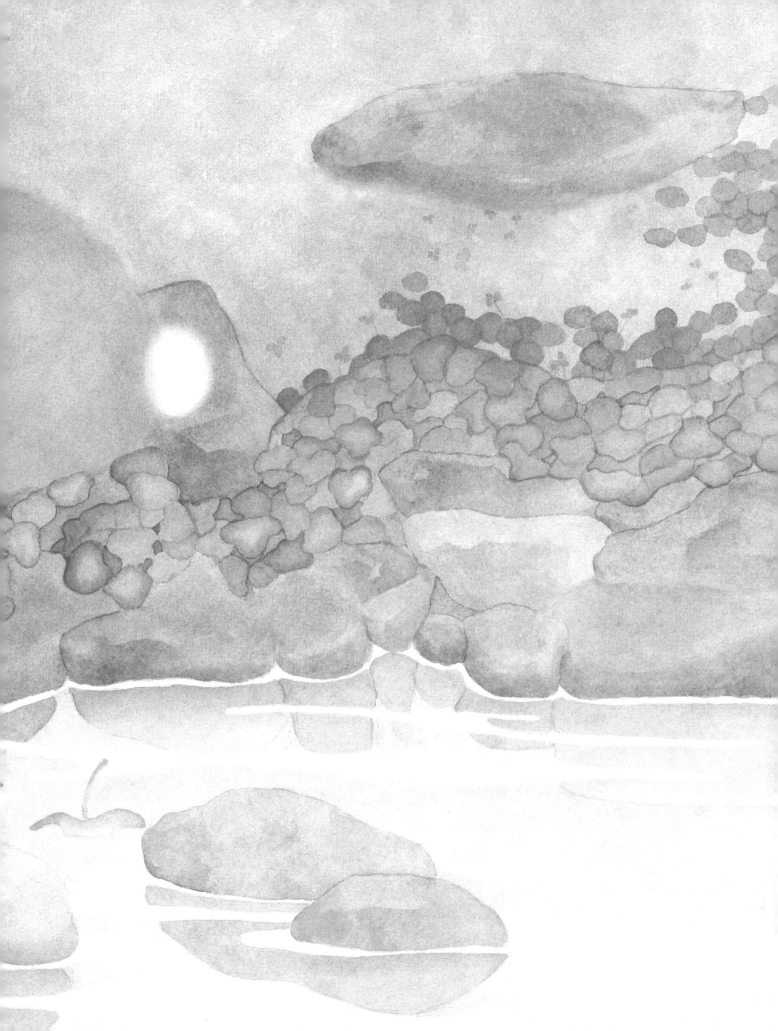

Little Cottontail laughed and twirled through sprinkles of sunlight until he grew tired. Then he lay beside the River, listening to the leaves high above.

"Listen, Mama. The Trees are singing. I think Grandfather is sending his summer song. I think he is singing to the Trees, far across the Meadow, and they are singing to each other, all the way to us."

Mama stopped in a patch of wild lettuce and listened.
"Yes. He always sang it when we were together."

Little Cottontail and Mama listened until orange and yellow sun ribbons touched the Earth. Mama Cottontail started to hop home. Little Cottontail hopped sleepily beside her.

Soon, the lights of a thousand Stars winked across the sky.

"Grandfather always winked at me when he tucked me into bed," said Little Cottontail. "I think Grandfather is winking to the Stars, so they can wink to me."

Mama kissed Little Cottontail's nose and nestled him into his soft, warm bed.

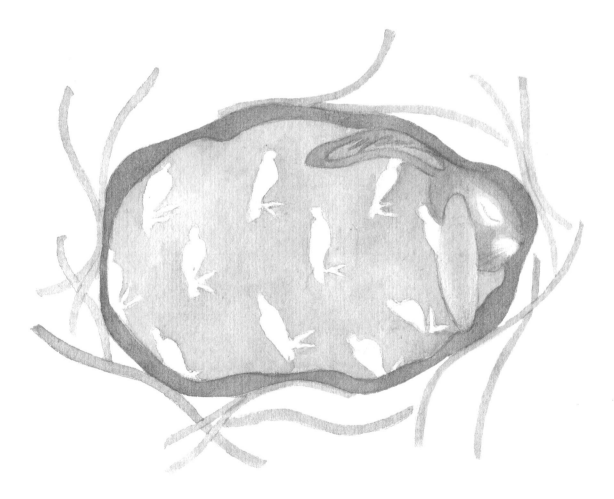

Little Cottontail looked deep into the Moon, hanging bright and bold in the sky.

"Let's blow our kisses high to the Moon, Mama, so the Moon can blow them to Grandfather."

Together, they blew kisses all the way to the Moon.

Then they dreamed of Wind hugs, Cloud smiles,
River jokes, and Tree songs, as Stars winked above and
Moon kisses floated down from the sky.